NEVER AGAIN!

Jasmine kept on thinking about the fall itself—the moment when she felt Outlaw hesitate at the jump . . . the moment when she realized she was out of rhythm with Outlaw . . . the moment when she knew she was going to fall. Worst of all, she kept on seeing, over and over again, the ground rushing up at her as she fell from the saddle.

"I can't ever go over a jump again," Jasmine said to herself. "But so what? Some people can't draw. Some people can't snap their fingers. I can't jump."

Jasmine and the Jumping Pony

B O N N I E   B R Y A N T

Illustrated by Marcy Ramsey

A SKYLARK BOOK
NEW YORK • TORONTO • LONDON • SYDNEY • AUCKLAND

RL 3, 007–010
JASMINE AND THE JUMPING PONY
A Bantam Skylark Book / February 1998

I would like to give my special thanks to Minna Jung for her help in the writing of this book.

Hi, we're the **PONY TAILS**—May Grover, Corey Takamura, and Jasmine James. We're neighbors, we're best friends, and most of all, we're pony-crazy.

My name is **May.** My pony is named Macaroni after my favorite food, macaroni and cheese. He's the sweetest pony in the world! He never loses his temper. Jasmine and Corey say he's the exact opposite of me. Of course, they're just teasing. I have two older sisters who say I'm a one-girl disaster area, but they're not teasing. Would you like some used sisters? I have two for sale.

I'm called **Corey**—short for Corinne. I live between Jasmine and May—in a lot of ways. My house is between theirs. I'm between them in personality, too. Jasmine's organized, May's forgetful, and I can be both. May's impulsive, Jasmine's cautious, and I'm just reasonable. My pony is named Samurai. He's got a white blaze on his face shaped like a samurai sword. Sam is temperamental, but he's mine and I love him.

I'm **Jasmine.** My pony is named Outlaw. His face is white, like an outlaw's mask. He can be as unpredictable as an outlaw, too, but I'd never let him go to jail because I love him to pieces! I like to ride him, and I also like to look after him. I have a baby sister named Sophie. When she gets older I'm going to teach her to ride.

So why don't you tack up and have fun with us on our pony adventures!

May Corey Jasmine

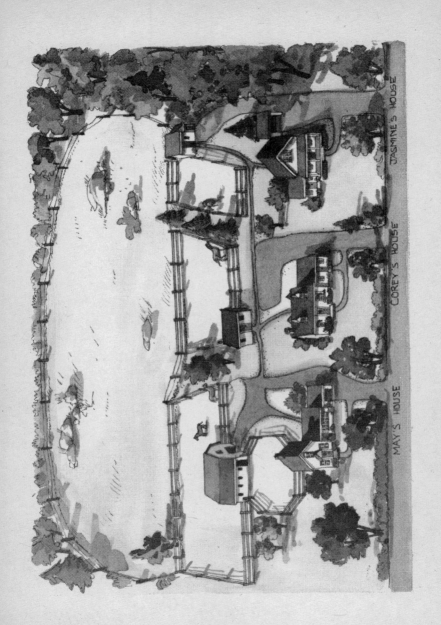

MAY'S HOUSE

COREY'S HOUSE

JASMINE'S HOUSE

Jasmine and the
Jumping Pony

1 A Busy Breakfast

Jasmine James finished brushing her long blond hair for school. She turned and looked again at the large poster lying on her desk.

For the past month, Jasmine's class at school had studied dinosaurs. Jasmine's teacher had asked each student to do a final project showing what he or she had learned.

Jasmine had decided to draw a poster that showed the different types of dinosaurs. Because she loved ponies, and loved to draw them, too, she also knew how to draw other animals.

The poster was divided into several sections. One section showed that some dinosaurs had skeletons that looked like the skeletons of birds and others had skeletons that looked like the skeletons of lizards. Another section showed that some dinosaurs were meat-eaters and others ate only plants. Everything was labeled in Jasmine's neat handwriting.

Jasmine had used every single color in her marker set and worked for hours and hours on her poster. Looking at it, she knew she had done a good job. But she felt slightly flat inside. She wasn't sure why. Then she heard her mother calling from downstairs.

"Jasmine, your breakfast is ready!" Mrs. James said.

Jasmine called back, "Be right down, Mom!"

She carefully rolled up her poster and taped a large piece of paper around it so that it wouldn't get dirty on the bus ride to school. Then she paused. If her poster was rolled up, her parents wouldn't be able to see it at breakfast.

Then she remembered what breakfast

was usually like these days. It was total chaos!

Lately, Jasmine's parents were so busy that they rushed through breakfast with Jasmine and Sophie, her baby sister, before hurrying off to work. Mrs. James, who was an artist, had missed a conference with Jasmine's teacher two days ago because Sophie had been slightly feverish that day. Now Mrs. James was working days and nights in her studio. She was trying to get ready for an exhibition in which her work would be shown along with the work of several other artists.

Mr. James, who worked for an environmental group, also seemed busier than usual. He was spending a lot of time at his office in Washington, D.C., and in his study at home. When he wasn't working, he took care of Sophie so that Mrs. James could get her work done.

Somehow Jasmine didn't feel right reminding her father that he had promised to take her and her two best friends, May and Corey, to a movie tonight.

Jasmine looked at her rolled-up poster

again. "They're probably too busy—I'll show it to them some other time," she told herself. She picked up the poster and her school bag and went downstairs.

On the way to the kitchen, Jasmine remembered something that cheered her up. Last night, May had called her and summoned the three Pony Tails—May, Jasmine, and Corey—to riding practice after school today.

The three girls called themselves the Pony Tails because they were best friends who loved to ride ponies. They lived next door to each other and belonged to the same pony club. The Pony Tails also had weekly riding lessons at the same stable, Pine Hollow.

The Pony Tails were so crazy about ponies that they took every opportunity to practice riding. Luckily, the winter in Virginia was really warm this year, warm enough to ride outdoors in the schooling ring next to May's house.

I'll practice my cantering, Jasmine thought. She had a big smile on her face as she went into the kitchen.

"Morning," she greeted her mother and

father. "Good morning," she whispered as she leaned over Sophie in her baby seat.

Mrs. James smiled at Jasmine. She looked tired. She plunked a bowl of oatmeal and a glass of orange juice in front of Jasmine. "Here, honey," she said. "I wanted to make French toast this morning, but I was up so late last night . . ." Her voice trailed off as Sophie started to whimper.

Mr. James was sitting at the table, drinking coffee and flipping through a thick three-ring notebook. He looked up and smiled at Jasmine. "Good morning, Jazzie," he said. He looked down at the notebook again.

Jasmine tucked her poster and school bag under her chair and sat down. No one had asked her about the poster.

She looked around for the brown sugar. Her mother knew she loved brown sugar on her oatmeal, and she usually put it on the table the days when they had oatmeal for breakfast.

But Jasmine didn't see any brown sugar on the table. She got up and found the

5

stepstool, then got the brown sugar from where it was kept above the sink.

Her mother was picking up Sophie and cooing to her. "Honey," she said to Mr. James, "I'm going to feed Sophie now. Then can you watch her for a few hours while I work this morning?"

Mr. James nodded. "I have to go into the office this afternoon, though. We have a big meeting," he said. "I won't be home until dinnertime, so maybe we should get a baby-sitter this afternoon."

Mrs. James sighed and shook her head. "No, I can handle it," she said. "Jasmine, where will you be?"

"Riding with the other Pony Tails," replied Jasmine. "Maybe I'll do something with them tonight, too," she added, looking at her father. She wondered if he would remember about the movie.

He just smiled absently at her, though, and said, "Great. Don't forget to call and let us know what you're doing."

"Have a good day at school, Jasmine!" called Mrs. James as she hurried into the den to nurse Sophie. Mr. James looked at his notebook again.

Jasmine finished her breakfast and placed her dishes neatly in the sink. She retrieved her poster and school bag from under the chair and went out to meet May and Corey at the bus stop.

I bet we can still do something fun together tonight, she thought. The Pony Tails almost always had a good time. The key ingredients, as they all knew, were their love of ponies and each other.

2 Jasmine Jumps Ahead

Jasmine, May, and Corey got off the bus after school and waved good-bye to their friends. May started jumping around. Unlike Jasmine and Corey, who were usually calm, May was always excited about something. Today she had a good reason.

"It's Friday!" she sang out.

Friday meant no school for two days. This Friday also meant that tomorrow, Saturday, the girls would go to Pine Hollow for a Pony Club meeting.

The three friends belonged to a Pony Club called Horse Wise. Horse Wise held a mounted meeting every other week. For mounted meetings, the Pony Tails brought their own ponies from home.

"Let's change and start practicing right away," suggested Corey.

"Oh yeah, don't forget—bring your ponies," added May.

Jasmine and Corey giggled. Then May put on a mock-stern expression and said, "We've got to work, work, work on our riding skills!"

This made them laugh even more. Even though practice was good for their riding skills, none of them considered it work. It was too much fun!

As Jasmine turned toward her house, Corey suddenly noticed the rolled-up poster under Jasmine's arm. "Hey, what's that?" she asked.

May noticed the poster, too. "Is that your dinosaur project?" she asked.

Jasmine shrugged. "It's nothing," she said. "Just a homework assignment."

Corey was about to ask Jasmine more questions, but May started jumping around impatiently again. "C'mon," she said. "We've got to get started—it gets

10

dark so early in the winter." The three girls ran off toward their houses.

When Jasmine got home, the house was quiet. She peeked into the den and saw her mother, lying asleep on the couch with Sophie curled up by her side. Sophie was fast asleep, too.

Jasmine tiptoed upstairs to her room. She set down her school bag and wondered where to put her dinosaur poster. Her teacher had loved it. She had asked Jasmine to bring it back for a school art exhibition in two weeks. In the meantime, Jasmine was supposed to keep it safe at home.

Jasmine wondered if her parents would be able to go the art exhibition. Then she remembered how busy they were these days. She quickly shoved the poster into her closet. She noticed that the edges had gotten a little bent by a pair of shoes.

She shrugged. It was just a poster.

She put on her riding clothes and went outside.

Outlaw, her pony, nickered when he saw her. "Hi, Outlaw," Jasmine said, giving him a hug. He shook his mane happily.

Unlike Jasmine, Outlaw had a mischievous, naughty streak—one that went with the banditlike white mask on his face, the reason for his name. Jasmine loved riding Outlaw, especially since he was always happy to spend time with her.

After tacking up, Jasmine rode over to May's house. Because May's father trained horses for a living, the Grovers' house had a large stable and two schooling rings in the back.

Corey was already there, mounted on her pony, Samurai. Corey had named him for the white, sword-shaped streak across his nose.

Jasmine could tell that Samurai was eager to start. He looked even friskier than usual. Since he was usually pretty lively, Corey had her hands full trying to get him to stand quietly.

"Hi," called Jasmine. Then May emerged from the stable, leading her pony, Macaroni—named because he was the color of May's favorite food, macaroni and cheese. May led Macaroni to the mounting block and swung into the saddle.

First, the three girls practiced their

12

gaits. To start, they concentrated on the slow trot, which helped them balance in the saddle. Then they worked on the posting trot, and then they moved from the posting trot into the canter.

Jasmine was having a great time. The biggest challenge in cantering was keeping your pony under control. Otherwise, the pony could break into a gallop. Outlaw, though, was behaving perfectly today. The three girls tried to keep in formation, single file, as if they were in riding class.

After a half hour of practicing, they stopped for a break. "That was great!" exclaimed Corey. Samurai, too, had been behaving perfectly.

"No, *we* were great," declared May. "I think our practice and lessons are really working!"

"I think we're getting to be good riders," Jasmine agreed.

"Me too," said May. "So I have an idea—why don't we try a few jumps?"

"I'm game," answered Corey immediately. Then May and Corey looked at Jasmine.

Jasmine felt a little nervous. "I haven't done that much jumping," she said. "Don't you think we should take a lesson with Max first?" Max Regnery was their riding teacher at Pine Hollow.

"We've already learned some stuff about jumping from Max," May reminded Jasmine. "And anyway, you *have* jumped before. Remember the big sister–little sister competition? You and Carole Hanson won first prize!"

Jasmine remembered how much fun that competition had been. She had been paired with Carole Hanson, one of the best riders at Pine Hollow and a member of the Saddle Club. The Saddle Club was an older group of girls who, like the Pony Tails, were best friends and loved riding. Jasmine and Carole had won the competition because of the last event, a jumping course.

Still Jasmine hesitated. "I don't know," she said. "Carole's so good, I think she won that competition for us."

"It's no big deal, Jazz," urged May. "You're good, too—Carole said so. It'll be fun, I promise!"

Jasmine gave in. "Okay," she agreed. "But nothing crazy."

Just then Mr. Grover walked out of the house. He smiled when he saw the girls.

"Hey, Dad," called May. "Can you help us set up for some jumps?"

"Sure," said Mr. Grover. He came over to the schooling ring. With his help, the Pony Tails dragged some cavalletti—long rails that hooked onto the approach side of a jump—into position.

Mr. Grover made sure the cavalletti were spaced evenly. "This helps the ponies get used to the idea of the rails and adjust their stride," he explained to the girls. They all nodded, having done this before with Max at Pine Hollow.

For several minutes the three girls took turns trotting over the rails. Jasmine concentrated hard on keeping Outlaw at an even pace so that he wouldn't hit the rails as he trotted over them.

"You're doing great!" called Mr. Grover. "Let's try something a little more difficult."

Mr. Grover raised the cavalletti slightly from the ground on blocks. May went first, then Corey, and then Jasmine. This time the ponies had to pick their feet up and step over the rails. The girls concentrated on keeping their heads up and their seats balanced.

Once again the exercise went perfectly. After her fourth try, May turned around and called back to Corey and Jasmine. She was grinning. "Hey, we're not so bad!" she said. "I think we're ready for some *real* jumping now. Let's try raising it three feet!"

Mr. Grover laughed. "Slow down, cowgirl," he told May. "But you're right, you are doing great. Let's try a little jump." He walked over and raised the cavalletti until they were six inches off the ground.

Jasmine felt an uncomfortable butterfly in her stomach. Jumping was a lot harder than regular riding. A rider had to tell her pony what to do. Even more importantly, the rider needed to stay with the pony throughout the jump. If she didn't, she was in danger of losing her balance.

Jasmine wanted to say no. She looked at May and Corey. Both of them were grin-

16

ning. She knew May was always excited about taking risks, but this time Corey looked eager to try jumping as well.

Both Corey and May had more jumping experience than Jasmine did. But she didn't want to look like a wimp in front of her best friends. So she took a deep breath and waited for her turn.

Corey went first. She loved jumping. She and Samurai had taken first prize in the pony hunter event at a recent horse show. Under Corey's guidance, Samurai sailed over the jumps.

"Good balance, Corey!" Mr. Grover called out.

Then May went. May was such a daredevil, she cantered Macaroni at the jumps a little too quickly. As a result, her form was not as good as Corey's. As she approached the jumps, her hands clenched tightly on the reins. She looked down at the ground instead of straight ahead. Macaroni sailed over the jumps anyway.

"This is so much fun!" May said as she trotted Macaroni back to wait for her next turn.

"Nice jumping, May, but keep your head

up," instructed Mr. Grover. "Don't look down; you need to guide the pony through the jump. Don't hold the reins so tightly. You've got to give Macaroni room to stretch his neck as he takes the jump." May nodded solemnly.

Jasmine gulped. She rode Outlaw to face the jumps and looked at Mr. Grover. He must have sensed her nervousness because he started talking again.

"Remember, Jasmine, most ponies love jumping," he said. "It's like playing a duet. You and Outlaw are such good friends, you should be able to tell him how to do this. Canter him slowly toward the jumps. Try to maintain your balance."

Jasmine nodded and started cantering toward the jumps. When she reached the first one, she leaned forward. She felt Outlaw gather himself and sail over the tiny jump. Then the second. Then the third. She'd done it!

As she cleared the last jump, Jasmine was startled by a burst of clapping and cheering from the edge of the ring. She looked over and saw her parents standing there, with Sophie fast asleep in her

stroller. They had watched the whole thing. "Great style, Jasmine!" Mrs. James called out. Mr. James whistled through his fingers.

May and Corey watched Jasmine, who was grinning happily, ride over to say hello to her parents. Then May turned to Corey. "What's the big deal?" she asked. "We've all jumped before with Horse Wise."

Corey shrugged. "Jasmine hasn't done that much jumping, I guess," she said. "But it's nice that her parents watch her do these things and cheer her on." Corey's parents were divorced. She lived with her mother, a veterinarian whom everyone called Doc Tock, short for Dr. Takamura. Corey got to see her father a lot, but she missed having her parents together.

May seemed to understand because she changed the subject. "Let's go say hi to Mr. and Mrs. James," she suggested.

Jasmine got to the edge of the ring where her parents were. "I didn't know you were watching. I thought you'd be working all afternoon," she said to them.

"I got a lot of work done today. But honey, I didn't know you were so good at jumping!" exclaimed Mrs. James.

"You looked like a real pro!" chimed in Mr. James.

Jasmine grinned again. She felt really good. She had been scared, but she had overcome her fear and made the jumps. More importantly, her parents had seen the whole thing and were really proud of her.

"Hey, Jazzie," said Mr. James. Jasmine was surprised to see her father looking a little bit sheepish, as if he had done something wrong.

"What, Dad?" she asked.

"After breakfast, I remembered that I promised to take you and the other Pony Tails to a movie tonight," Mr. James said. "And then I remembered that I forgot all about the promise!"

By this time May and Corey, along with Mr. Grover, had reached Jasmine's parents. Everyone said hello, and then Mr. James kept on talking.

"I'm sorry I forgot about the movie," he said. "But I'm really too tired to do it tonight, it's been such a long day. How about renting *National Velvet* and having a Pony Tails sleepover instead?"

May, Corey, and Jasmine turned to each other and said at the same time, "Cool!" Then they gave each other a high five and exclaimed "Jake!" That was what they always did when they said the same thing at exactly the same time.

Not only a day, but a night thinking about ponies. What could be better?

Best of all, thought Jasmine happily, my parents will be there, too.

3 Jasmine Makes a Decision

May stuffed a handful of buttery popcorn into her mouth. "That was great," she announced with her mouth full.

Corey, sitting next to May, agreed. "That was one of the best movies I've ever seen," she said.

National Velvet was over. After a dinner of salad and pizza, the three Pony Tails had settled themselves on the couch in the Jameses' den and watched the whole movie. None of them had seen it before.

They were thrilled by the story. The plot involved a young girl who disguised herself as a boy so that she could ride her horse in the National, one of the biggest horse races in England. The National looked like a really tough race. It was a steeplechase, which meant that the horses not only had to run, but also had to go over huge jumps.

"Imagine," said May dreamily. "Dressing up as a boy *and* getting to ride in that race."

"Don't get any ideas, May," warned Mr. James. Everyone laughed.

Mr. James had watched the movie with them. After putting Sophie down to sleep, Mrs. James had watched the movie, too. She had also contributed some of her famous cookies, along with a bowl of popcorn and glasses of juice. The Pony Tails were in heaven. Next to riding, this was the best kind of fun in the world.

"It gets better every time I see it," commented Mrs. James. She smiled at Jasmine. "That young girl, flying over those jumps in the race! It reminded me of you, the way you took those jumps today."

"Flying Jazzie!" put in Mr. James.

Jasmine blushed, but she was pleased.

May said, "Those jumps were really tiny. I think we can do better than that."

"Samurai was definitely ready for more," said Corey.

Mr. James yawned. "Well, there's only one thing I'm ready for, and that's sleep," he declared. "Upstairs, young ladies. Don't forget to brush your teeth."

Jasmine's room had two beds in it, and Jasmine's mother brought in the guest cot. Jasmine volunteered to sleep on the cot, since May and Corey were her guests. They all brushed their teeth and climbed into bed.

After the light was turned out, Jasmine spoke. "Are you asleep yet?"

"Mmm," mumbled May.

"What's up, Jazz?" asked Corey.

"It's about ponies," teased Jasmine.

"I'm awake," said May. They all giggled—softly, so that they wouldn't wake up Jasmine's parents or Sophie.

"I've been thinking," continued Jasmine. "I've decided to sign up for a jumping class at Pine Hollow."

"That's a great idea, Jazz," May said sleepily.

"It's always good to add new skills," Corey told Jasmine.

"Don't you want to join, too?" asked Jasmine.

"Not this year," said Corey. "I love riding, but I also love helping my mom out with her veterinary work. An extra riding lesson would give me less time to do that."

Jasmine understood. She and May both knew that Corey was thinking of becoming a veterinarian someday, just like her mom.

"May?" asked Jasmine. But all she heard was a muffled "Mmmph, too busy, maybe later." So Jasmine and Corey knew that May was well on her way to sleep.

"We'll cheer you on," promised Corey.

"Thanks," said Jasmine. "I guess we really should get to sleep, since we have a mounted meeting tomorrow."

Corey said good night. Soon after, Jasmine heard her breathing evenly.

Jasmine couldn't sleep for a while. She was happy that May and Corey liked her idea. They always encouraged her to try new things. That was why she loved being friends with them.

She was especially excited about telling

her parents tomorrow. Judging from their reaction today, they would be even prouder when they heard about the jumping class. They'll definitely want to see me perform in shows, thought Jasmine.

Thinking of high jumps and blue ribbons, she fell asleep.

*   *   *

The next morning Jasmine woke up very early. She looked at Corey, who was still fast asleep. Then she looked at May. Her face was still buried in her pillow. She was also fast asleep!

Jasmine couldn't sleep another wink. She was too excited about jumping. She got out of bed and went to see if her parents were awake.

First she peered into her parents' bedroom. She could see her father, still fast asleep. What a bunch of sleepyheads! Jasmine thought.

Then she heard a sound from the bathroom down the hallway. She found her mother giving Sophie a bath. A delicious smell was wafting its way upstairs.

Mrs. James smiled when she saw Jasmine. "Good morning, honey," she said. "You're up early for a Saturday."

"Mom, I've decided to take a jumping class at Pine Hollow," Jasmine blurted out. "I really want to learn as much about jumping as I can, if that's okay with you and Dad."

Mrs. James didn't answer for a second. She was busy turning Sophie over so that she could carefully wash her back. Jasmine knew, from helping her mother with this task, how slippery Sophie could get in the water. It was like trying to wash a jumping bean!

"Ooopsy-daisy," said Mrs. James. Then she looked up at Jasmine. "Okay," she said. "We'll see what can be worked out."

Jasmine took that as a yes. She ran back to her room.

"Wake up, wake up!" she said. She sat down on May's bed, and on May's foot by accident.

"Ouch," grumbled May sleepily. Then she looked at Jasmine. "What's up, Jazz? You're acting more like me this morning."

Jasmine giggled. It was true. Normally

May was the one who crashed and bumped into things. Jasmine usually took her time.

Corey yawned and stretched. "I was having the most wonderful dream, about winning the National on Samurai," she said. Then she, too, looked at Jasmine. "What's up? You look like you're about to burst."

"Mom said okay to an extra jumping class," Jasmine told them happily. "I can hardly wait to tell Max."

"That's great," said May. She sat up and stretched. "Speaking of Max, it's a good thing you woke us up. It's Saturday—you know what that means!"

Corey and Jasmine nodded. Saturday, of course, meant a Horse Wise meeting at Pine Hollow.

"I have to go help my father get the trailer ready," said May, jumping out of bed. For mounted meetings, Mr. Grover brought their own ponies from home.

"I wanted to give Samurai an extra-special grooming this morning," said Corey, also climbing out of bed.

"Blueberry muffins, girls!" called Mrs.

James from downstairs. That explained the delicious smell.

The three girls looked at each other.

"Well, maybe we can eat first," suggested Jasmine.

May and Corey agreed. They quickly finished dressing and followed their noses downstairs.

4 Jasmine Signs Up

The morning was beautiful. Jasmine had tacked up Outlaw in record time. She wanted a chance to speak to Max before class.

As she waited by the door that led to the schooling ring, she reached up and touched the good-luck horseshoe. The horseshoe was a tradition at Pine Hollow and was supposed to prevent riders from getting hurt.

She saw Max walking toward the schooling ring. "Max!" she called out.

He turned and saw her. "Hi, Jasmine. You're early today." Jasmine knew Max liked it when students arrived promptly for riding class and club meetings.

"What's on your mind, Jasmine?" Max asked.

"I want to take a jumping class," Jasmine told him. "We practiced riding the other day, and we did a few jumps. I think Outlaw really liked it."

Max smiled. He was a tough but fair teacher, and his compliments were rare. Whenever one of the Pony Tails received praise from Max, it made her day.

"That's a really good idea," Max told Jasmine. "Even though I always stress learning the basics, I think it's equally important to stretch yourself and take on new challenges. This afternoon, we'll give you and Outlaw a test to see what jumping class you should take."

Jasmine nodded. "I'll be ready."

Max nodded cheerfully and walked into the schooling ring. Corey and May joined Jasmine at the horseshoe. Then Max asked everyone to warm up their ponies.

Normally Jasmine loved riding with Horse Wise, but today she could barely concentrate. She trotted when she should have walked. When they began cantering, she lost a stirrup because she wasn't keeping her heels down. Max had to remind her several times to sit up straight.

Jasmine got more and more nervous about the jump test. Suppose Outlaw didn't behave? Suppose she and Outlaw ended up in a baby jumping class?

Even though Jasmine had barely any jumping experience, she didn't think she belonged in a baby jumping class. "I've got to do well on the test," she told herself.

"Jasmine!" Max called out, exasperated. "Why are you holding the reins so tightly? You know better than that."

Jasmine flushed. She loosened her grip on the reins. She knew she was communicating her nervousness to Outlaw.

After the class, Max asked Jasmine to wait in the ring. He talked to a few of the Horse Wise members and their parents. In the meantime, Corey and May unsaddled their ponies and came back to watch.

Corey turned to May. "I touched the

horseshoe on my way back in, for Jasmine," she said.

May nodded. "Good idea. Jazz is really nervous, I can tell. I hope she does well."

They leaned against the fence to watch. Max quickly lined up some cavalletti on the ground. Then he asked Jasmine to walk Outlaw over the cavalletti. Jasmine did it perfectly. Max asked her to do the same thing several more times. Then he asked her to trot over the cavalletti. Again Jasmine did it perfectly.

"This is just like our practice," said May to Corey.

"Shhh," said Corey. "I think he's going to raise the jumps now."

Sure enough, Max raised three jumps six inches off the ground. They were set at intervals in the center of the ring. "Try these, Jasmine," he called out.

Jasmine trotted Outlaw back to face the jumps. Her expression was calm, and she cantered Outlaw easily toward the jumps. May and Corey were impressed with how poised Jasmine looked.

Jasmine wasn't feeling poised on the inside, though. She felt really nervous, but she tried not to show it in front of Max, May, and Corey.

She sailed over the first jump, then the second, then the third. She leaned forward at just the right moment, and she and Outlaw landed together perfectly.

"Good job, Jasmine!" Max said approvingly. He motioned for her to follow him to the edge of the ring.

When Jasmine and Outlaw got to the edge of the ring, Max started talking. "Outlaw seems to be a natural jumper," he said. "Also, Jasmine, I'm pleased with how much you've worked on your balance and hand position. If you work hard, you could be good at jumping. I have a jumping lesson for beginners to intermediates that meets on Wednesdays, right after your regular riding class. But you'll need to learn with your own pony—it's hard to learn by jumping on a different pony every week."

Jasmine turned and looked at May in dismay. For their weekday lessons, the Pony Tails usually left their ponies at home. On those days, they rode Pine Hollow ponies. It was too much to ask Mr.

Grover to bring their ponies to Pine Hollow on weekdays *and* weekends.

May nodded. "Don't worry, Jazz," she said. "I'll talk to my dad about it. He'll say yes, especially since it's only one pony."

Jasmine felt reassured. When May looked that determined, she usually got what she wanted. "Thanks, May," Jasmine said.

Jasmine couldn't stop smiling. She and Outlaw had really impressed Max! She was a little disappointed that the class was for beginners as well as intermediates. Surely with intermediate-level jumpers in the class, Max would let them try some higher jumps.

When Mr. Grover came to pick up the ponies and the girls, May asked him immediately about the Wednesday class. He looked at Jasmine with a grin. "Bitten by the jumping bug, eh?" he asked. "I remember feeling exactly the same way about jumping, so how can I say no?"

"Did I ever tell you that you're my favorite dad, Dad?" May said.

He waved a hand. "Flattery will get

you everywhere, daughter dear." Jasmine thanked Mr. Grover again and again, until he told her she was hurting his ears.

"C'mon, everyone, let's go home!" he said.

When Jasmine got to her house, she led Outlaw into his stable and fed and watered him. Most days, Jasmine liked to take as long as possible with this task. Today, however, she raced through it.

Outlaw looked hurt. "Sorry, Outlaw," said Jasmine, kissing his nose. "I've got to tell Mom and Dad the news."

She ran inside and found her parents at the table. Her dad took one look at her and started to laugh. "I know you love riding, Jazzie," he said, "but you look like you've just won the biggest prize in the world!"

"Mom, Dad, I'm taking a jumping class on Wednesdays," Jasmine told them. "I tried out for Max today, and he said I did really well. He said Outlaw was a natural jumper."

Mrs. James looked surprised. "I didn't think this would happen so quickly!" she exclaimed. "I thought we were going to talk more after this morning!"

"Talk more about what?" asked Mr. James. He looked thoroughly confused. "What did you talk about this morning?"

Jasmine and Mrs. James filled him in on Jasmine's new love of jumping. When he finally understood that Jasmine had already signed up for a jumping class, and that Mr. Grover was going to take Outlaw to Pine Hollow, he shook his head.

"You certainly don't let the grass grow under your feet, do you?" he said to Jasmine.

"That means you acted very quickly," clarified Mrs. James.

"Yes, but I really want to do this!" said Jasmine. "I think I could be really good at it!"

"Isn't jumping much more dangerous than regular riding?" asked Mrs. James.

Jasmine took a deep breath. "Some people do get hurt, but you know how careful I always am about riding, Mom," she said.

Mr. and Mrs. James had to agree. Jasmine observed every safety precaution when she rode. She checked her riding gear before every ride and wore a hard hat that was approved by the U.S. Pony Club. She never rode alone, and she always touched the good-luck horseshoe before she went riding.

"Please, Mom, Dad, there's nothing to worry about," Jasmine pleaded. "Don't you think I can do this?"

This made her parents smile. "Of course we think you can do it," said Mr. James. "Not only that, but I admire your courage and determination in *wanting* to do it. You have our permission, as long as Mr. Grover doesn't mind taking Outlaw to class on Wednesdays."

Jasmine glowed. Her parents were proud of her now, but wait until they saw her really jump! She could hardly wait until the first show where she could jump in an event.

Maybe I'll compete in a race like the National someday! she thought.

5 Pony Tail Art

On Sunday afternoon, May and Jasmine headed to Corey's house. Corey had called them up and simply said, "I need help—please come over." So of course they rushed over right away.

They found Corey in her room, surrounded by wrinkled pieces of oaktag. When she saw May and Jasmine, Corey sighed in relief. "Thank goodness you're here!"

May flopped down on the floor, accidentally sitting on several sheets of oaktag. It didn't seem to matter—most of them were scribbled on and wrinkled anyway. She began pulling them out from un-

der her and inspecting them. "What are you doing?" she asked.

Corey made a face. "I volunteered to draw a poster for my mom's office, showing all the different kinds of animals she works with. Only I can't seem to get it right!"

Jasmine picked up a piece of oaktag from the bed. "This German shepherd looks fine," she told Corey soothingly.

"Yes, but look at the cat next to it," wailed Corey. "Notice anything strange?"

"We-e-ell, yes," said Jasmine hesitantly. "It looks a lot . . . bigger than the dog."

"Here." Corey handed Jasmine another piece of oaktag. "I started drawing a parakeet in the bottom right-hand corner. But after I drew its head, I didn't know where to put the tail! If I put the tail in the right place, it would go right off the paper!"

May couldn't help giggling. Corey, who was usually so sensible and logical, looked like a mad scientist. Her neat black hair was messed up, and she had a wild look in her eyes.

Jasmine, though, started briskly picking up pieces of oaktag. "Look, Corey, I can help you," she said. "I just did a chart for school. There are things you can do that make drawing a whole lot easier. Just wait a sec and I'll be right back."

She dashed out of the room. Corey looked hopefully at May, who shrugged in puzzlement.

Jasmine reappeared two minutes later. She was carrying her marker set and her large sketchpad. "Look, here's what I do," she said. "First you make a draft on a large piece of paper. That way, you don't waste too many pieces of good oaktag. I always use pencil, and I press really lightly, so I can erase if I want to change the design.

"Also," she continued, "I divide the design into different sections. If you work in smaller sections, it's easier to keep everything in proportion.

"Finally," she concluded, "I copy the design onto the oaktag. Then I color in everything. That's the final step."

May jumped up. "I have an idea!" she said. "Why don't I borrow some veterinary magazines from your mom so we can copy from the pictures?" She ran out of the room.

When May came back with an armful of magazines, the three girls set to work. Using the magazine pictures, Jasmine helped Corey sketch a draft of the poster onto the pad. Then Corey and Jasmine carefully copied the design onto a clean piece of oaktag. Finally May, Corey, and Jasmine colored in all the animals, using Jasmine's markers.

When they were finished, they stared in awe at their work. The poster was beautiful!

"I think we could have a business doing posters," declared May. "Let's be professional riders, with a poster-design business on the side!"

Corey shook her head. "No, Jasmine's the one with the talent," she said.

May nodded. "How did you know what to do?" she asked Jasmine. "Did your mother show you?"

Jasmine shrugged. "Practice makes perfect, I guess—just like in riding. I had to do a chart for my dinosaur project, too."

Both May and Corey looked at Jasmine then. "Were you carrying the dinosaur poster on Friday?" demanded May.

"Why didn't you show it to us, Jazz?" asked Corey.

Jasmine shrugged again. "It's no big deal, really," she said. "I've got it at home. Maybe I'll show it to you sometime."

Jasmine usually liked showing her friends her pictures. Now she didn't want to talk about it. Corey and May looked at each other and shrugged also. Then they let the subject drop.

6 Jasmine's First Jumping Class

Jasmine thought Wednesday would never come. She could think about nothing else but the jumping class.

At school she could barely concentrate. When her teacher asked her to work out a math problem on the blackboard, Jasmine got it wrong.

Her teacher gave her another problem, and Jasmine got that one wrong, too. She had done the problems okay last night. Now she couldn't remember anything.

"It's not like you, Jasmine, to make mistakes," her teacher said. She shook her head and excused Jasmine from the blackboard.

Jasmine returned to her seat. All she could think about was jumping. She could already feel the wind in her hair and see how the breeze rippled through Outlaw's mane as he soared over high jumps. She could see the blue ribbons lined up on her bedroom shelf. Or maybe she'd put them on the wall.

Deep down inside, Jasmine knew it took long years of practice and hard work before a rider could jump well. But she felt sure that she and Outlaw were on their way toward that goal.

After school, Doc Tock took the Pony Tails to their weekly riding lesson. Each week the parents of the Pony Tails took turns driving the three girls to Pine Hollow. Mr. Grover would bring Outlaw later, after their regular lesson.

Once again, Jasmine had trouble focusing during class. When Max asked everyone to practice changing gaits, Jasmine gave the signals either too early or too late. She didn't pay as much attention as she should have to Max's directions.

Luckily, she was riding Peso, one of the

Pine Hollow ponies. All the Pine Hollow ponies were named for small change. Peso was so experienced that Jasmine's mistakes weren't as noticeable as they could have been. Whenever Jasmine seemed confused, Peso followed the lead of the other ponies in class.

Then it was time for the jumping class.

Corey and May waved good-bye as Mr. Grover pulled up with Outlaw. "Good luck, Jazz!" they called.

It made Jasmine feel good to hear her best friends wish her luck. She was sorry Corey and May couldn't stay, but Corey wanted to help her mom take care of some animals. May was going shopping with her mother. Normally May hated shopping, unlike Jasmine, who loved clothes. Today was her big sister Dottie's birthday, though, and May wanted to find a present. As usual, May had left the present-shopping until the last minute.

Then again, Jasmine was relieved to see them go. Sometimes being watched when she tried something new made her nervous.

"I'll be back in forty-five minutes," promised Mr. Grover after he had unloaded Outlaw.

Jasmine took Outlaw into the stable and put on his saddle and bridle. She swung into the saddle and remembered to touch the horseshoe before heading for the schooling ring.

"Not that way, Jasmine!" called Max. "We have to warm up first in the indoor ring."

Jasmine recognized most of the other riders in the class. A few girls were from Horse Wise, including Jackie Rogers. For about fifteen minutes, the riders circled the indoor ring, first at a walk, then at a trot, and then at a slow canter.

Jasmine was disappointed. This class was just like the regular Wednesday class!

Finally Max led them into the outdoor ring. Jasmine could see the cavalletti laid out flat on the ground, just the way Mr. Grover had laid them out on Friday.

First Max had them walk over the cavalletti. Then he asked them to trot over the cavalletti, so that the ponies could adjust their stride.

Jasmine frowned. They were doing exactly the same stuff that she, May, and Corey had practiced on Friday!

She fidgeted. Max saw her. "Jasmine, keep your heels down and your toes in!" he called out sternly. Sure enough, Jasmine's feet were resting loosely against the stirrups.

Then Max had them do a strange exercise. He asked them to trot slowly toward the cavalletti. When they got to the cavalletti, they were supposed to drop their reins and spread their arms. As soon as the ponies stepped over the rail, they could pick up the reins again.

"This will teach you about balance and confidence," Max explained. "Keep your upper bodies as straight as possible. It will also teach you to guide your ponies without using the reins too much."

Jasmine didn't do very well at the exercise. She could feel her body wobbling from side to side. Still, Outlaw stepped perfectly over the rails.

"You have to sit up straighter, Jasmine," said Max. "If you don't have the correct posture to begin with, you won't be able to lean forward and give your pony the signal to jump. Fortunately, Outlaw really seems to be a natural at this," Max added as Outlaw trotted back to the end of the line.

Jasmine barely heard Max. When were they going to start jumping?

At last Max asked the students to help pick up the cavalletti. It was time to jump!

7 First Jump

The first jump was ready. It was only six inches high, and Jasmine was surprised. Surely they could start with something more exciting!

The students lined up to take the jump. Jasmine was last in line. She was upset about the low jump.

Jasmine and Corey and May loved to watch horse shows on television, and Jasmine knew that jumps could be as much as six feet high. If Max raised the bar only six inches per class, how long would it take before Jasmine and Outlaw could jump six feet?

She was startled out of her calculations by Max's voice. "Jasmine, your turn!"

Without preparing herself, Jasmine began cantering Outlaw toward the jump. In her mind she could see her future, made up of six-foot jumps and blue ribbons.

Suddenly the jump ahead looked awfully high.

Jasmine blinked. Her heart started to pound. She felt Outlaw speed up, and she realized what was about to happen. Outlaw was going to *jump*. All four of his feet were going to leave the ground, which meant that she and Outlaw were going to be standing on *nothing but air*.

How was she going to hang on? What had made her think she could do this?

About ten feet in front of the jump, Jasmine leaned almost flat against Outlaw's neck. She tightened the reins and gripped them as hard as she could.

Outlaw was confused. He knew the jump was still ten feet away, so why was Jasmine leaning over, telling him to jump now? Why was she tightening the reins? Why was she acting as if an enormous jump were directly ahead?

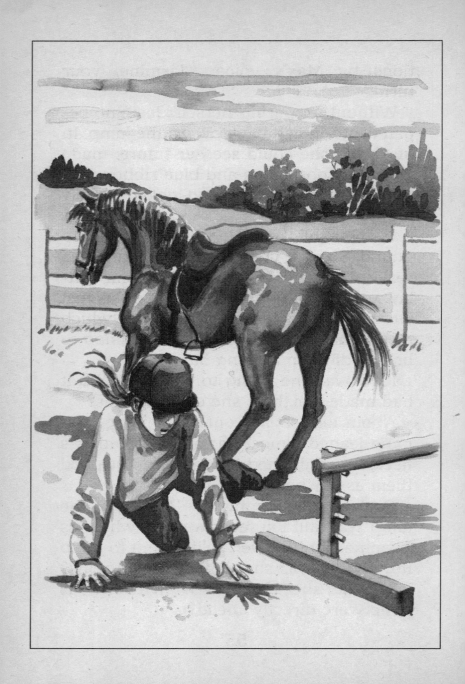

Outlaw usually trusted Jasmine completely, but he was a smart pony. He could see it was only a six-inch jump.

He slowed down little by little. When he reached the jump, he almost stopped. At the last minute, he gave a short, jerky hop and popped over the jump.

Jasmine, who had prepared for the jump far too early, was not ready for Outlaw's little hop when it came. Because she was leaning so far over Outlaw's neck, she was unable to regain her balance. As Outlaw landed, she fell off his back.

Immediately she rolled away from Outlaw. Max had taught his students to roll out of the way to avoid being accidentally stepped on by the ponies. Fortunately, the dirt in the ring was soft.

Max rushed over to Jasmine. Several other students dismounted and followed.

"Are you okay, Jasmine?" Max asked. He sounded concerned. He bent down and examined Jasmine for broken bones. When he found none, he helped her get to her feet.

The other students made sympathetic

noises. Jackie Rogers helped Jasmine brush the dirt off her clothes.

Jasmine couldn't speak. Her shoulder was a little sore where she had landed, but she didn't feel as if she'd even have much of a bruise.

What she did feel was hot, burning disappointment. She felt embarrassed. How could she daydream about six-foot jumps when she couldn't even clear six inches?

Max attempted to cheer her up. "You're fine, kiddo," he told her. Then he went and got Outlaw, who was patiently standing about ten feet away. Max led Outlaw back to Jasmine and gave her the signal to remount.

Jasmine didn't move.

"Jasmine, everyone takes a fall now and then," Max reminded her. "If you're not hurt, the best thing is to get right back on your pony. Riding well has a lot to do with confidence."

Jasmine still didn't move. Jackie said, "C'mon, Jasmine, you'll be fine." Other students encouraged Jasmine to get back on. Jasmine shook her head.

"Everyone falls off ponies," Max told Jasmine.

"Not me," said Jasmine. "Never again."
She took Outlaw's reins from Max and walked back to the stable. "I'm never going to jump again," she told herself.

8 Corey and May Step In

Both Corey and May heard about Jasmine's fall from Jasmine herself. She had briefly described the fall, then finished with, "And that's the end of jumping for me. I can ride, but I can't jump. I won't jump."

Corey and May tried to reason with her, but Jasmine wouldn't say another word.

On the Friday after Jasmine's fall, May made a suggestion while they were riding home on the bus. "Let's get together and practice riding this afternoon," she said.

Jasmine was uncharacteristically slow to agree. "I have a big school project," she said.

May gave an exasperated sigh. "It's Friday, Jazz! You have two whole days to do schoolwork!"

"Remember how much fun last Friday was?" Corey added.

"Okay," Jasmine agreed. "But no jumping." They got off the bus at their stop, and Jasmine walked away.

May and Corey watched Jasmine walk toward her house. "Corey, I've been thinking," May began.

Corey held up her hand. "You don't have to tell me."

"Jazz is afraid. We've got to help her!" announced May.

Corey grinned. May always wanted to help people. But then Corey's face got serious. "Jasmine's such a good rider," she said. "She should try jumping again. We've got to do something."

"We'll try not to be obvious," said May. "We'll just sort of suggest the idea of jumping to her. Again . . . and again . . . and again . . . and again."

Corey laughed. She knew how persistent May could be!

* * *

61

The three girls met up at the Grovers' schooling ring. They began their practice the same way as the week before. For a few minutes they concentrated on warming their ponies up by walking, trotting, and cantering.

Once she'd started riding Outlaw, Jasmine began to feel happy again. She loved riding Outlaw. She knew how to do it. She just wouldn't jump ever again.

Then May dismounted from Macaroni and set up a little jump. "How about some jumping practice? You first, Jazz," she said, pointedly looking at Jasmine.

"Yeah, go for it!" encouraged Corey.

Jasmine flushed. "I told you guys, I'm never jumping again!" she said. Her voice sounded sharp—very different from the way she usually talked to her best friends.

May was quiet. Then she shrugged and suggested, "How about Follow the Leader?"

The Pony Tails loved to play this game while riding. They decided Corey would be the leader.

Jasmine didn't pay much attention to the game, although she followed Corey automatically. Jasmine was embarrassed by the way she had spoken to May and Corey. She knew they only wanted to help her.

But Jasmine had done a lot of thinking since Wednesday's jumping class. She realized that one of the reasons she had been so excited about the jumping class was that her parents had seemed so enthusiastic about her jumping.

I was only trying to get their attention, she thought. That's not a good reason to do anything.

More than that, though, Jasmine kept on thinking about the fall itself—the moment when she felt Outlaw hesitate at the jump . . . the moment when she realized she was out of rhythm with Outlaw . . . the moment when she knew she was going to fall. Worst of all, she kept on seeing, over and over again, the ground rushing up at her as she fell from the saddle.

"I can't ever go over a jump again," Jasmine said to herself. "But so what? Some people can't draw. Some people can't snap their fingers. I can't jump.

"But," she added to herself, patting Outlaw's neck, "I can still ride Outlaw."

*　　*　　*

After their riding practice, May called Corey on the phone. "I don't think our strategy is going to work," she began.

"No," sighed Corey. "If we keep on suggesting jumps to Jazz, she'll just get mad at us."

"I was talking to my dad today, after our practice," said May. "He said it's really hard for riders to get their confidence back if they've had a bad experience."

"I don't think we should try to make Jazz do anything she doesn't want to do," argued Corey.

"It's not that," May said emphatically. "I'm not saying Jazz has to jump! It's just that jumping is fun, and I *know* Jazz can do it. She's a good rider. My dad said so. He also said Outlaw was born to jump. Jasmine could really do well on him if she'd just give it another chance."

Corey was silent. Then she said, "You're right, May. Anyway, we're Jasmine's best friends. We should be able to help her get through this."

"What can we do?" asked May.

Corey thought for a second. "Remember when I was so frustrated about that animal poster? Remember how I asked you and Jasmine for help? You guys had great ideas. Jasmine showed me how to sketch the poster first. Then you suggested the magazine pictures. Why do you think the poster turned out so well?"

It was May's turn to think. "We're geniuses?" she said hopefully.

"No," said Corey patiently. "Think again."

May thought hard. "Teamwork?" she guessed.

"Exactly," said Corey triumphantly.

"We've got to take this step by step," decided May.

"We've got to have a plan," said Corey.

They started to brainstorm.

*   *   *

Saturday's Horse Wise meeting was an unmounted one. This meant that the girls left their ponies at home. Max taught them a few new things about taking care of their horses. After the meeting, Jas-

65

mine tacked up Outlaw and rode over to the Grovers' schooling ring. She looked around suspiciously for jumps that either May or Corey had set up.

She didn't see any jumps in the ring. Instead she saw Corey, sitting on Samurai. A few seconds later May rode up on Macaroni.

"Ready?" said May.

For the next hour the girls practiced in the schooling ring. They tried to practice what they had learned in their Wednesday lesson with their own ponies.

May and Corey were careful not to mention jumping to Jasmine. May clowned around. She told a lot of her crazy jokes, which made Jasmine laugh.

Corey laughed at May's jokes, too. She also took the time to compliment Jasmine on her riding.

After an hour of practice, May suggested a ride across the field behind their houses. The Pony Tails were allowed to ride short distances if at least one other person was present, and the people who owned the field didn't mind when the girls rode across it.

Jasmine was having a wonderful time. For the first time since Wednesday, she stopped thinking about her fall. She was just happy to be riding Outlaw with her best friends.

It was a mild winter day, almost like spring. "This is the most beautiful day," Jasmine said happily to May and Corey.

"I agree," said May. When Jasmine wasn't looking, she winked at Corey.

Phase one of their plan was working. Jasmine seemed relaxed for the first time since the jumping class.

9 May and Corey Help Out

The next day, in the early afternoon, a knock came at the Jameses' back door. "I'll get it," said Jasmine. She got up from the kitchen table, where she had been making funny faces at Sophie. The remains of a huge Sunday brunch were on the table.

May and Corey were standing outside. They were dressed in riding clothes. "Come riding with us," invited May.

Jasmine turned and looked at her parents. "Go ahead," said her father. "Although," he added with a groan, "I don't know how you can do anything. I just ate six waffles—all I'm ready for is a long nap."

The Pony Tails giggled. Jasmine ran upstairs to change into her riding clothes.

After tacking up Outlaw, the three girls strolled over to the Grovers' with Jasmine leading Outlaw by the reins. May and Corey told her Macaroni and Samurai were ready to go, waiting at the Grovers'.

"By the way," said Corey casually, "May and I want to work on some jumps. Don't worry," she added quickly as Jasmine looked at her in alarm. "We know the drill. No jumps for you ever again. But maybe you can help us set up the jumps, okay?"

Jasmine agreed. She certainly knew how to do that, and she never minded helping her friends.

When they got to May's house, she saw Mr. Grover, working in the ring next to theirs with a student horse. The horse was learning how to walk on a lead line, and Mr. Grover had his hands full.

"We're going to do some jumps, Dad," May called out.

"I'll keep an eye on you, but I can't help you right now," Mr. Grover replied.

After a few minutes of riding, May and Corey set up some small jumps with Jasmine's help. Jasmine continued to practice trotting and cantering around the ring. She concentrated on her hand and leg positions.

Out of the corner of her eye, she saw May take Macaroni over the jumps. Then it was Corey's turn.

To Jasmine's surprise, Corey seemed to be having trouble with Samurai. When May and Jasmine had first met Corey, Samurai had been a mischievous pony and not as well trained as Macaroni and Outlaw. But under Corey's patient guidance, Samurai had been getting better and better.

Today, though, he seemed more like his old self. He balked when Corey approached the first jump. He finally went over the rail, but he broke out of his canter and simply trotted over the second and third jumps. Jasmine stopped to watch. This was the only time she had

ever seen Corey and Samurai mess up at jumping together.

Then Corey rode over to Jasmine. She looked discouraged. "I guess Sam's just in one of his moods today," she said.

"I can't believe it," said Jasmine. "He's been so good."

Corey shook her head. "He still gets into his moods, and when he does, there's nothing I can do." She paused for a second, then said, "Hey, Jasmine, I really want to practice today. Would you mind if I borrowed Outlaw?"

Jasmine nodded. She knew how much Corey loved jumping. She dismounted, and Corey took her place. Jasmine held Samurai by the reins.

Corey swung Outlaw around and cantered toward the jumps. Outlaw sailed over them smoothly. Corey's face was one big grin.

Watching Outlaw and Corey, Jasmine felt proud of her pony. Outlaw had such a smooth canter, and he took the jumps with a lot of spirit.

Then May and Macaroni went again. This time it didn't go quite as smoothly as the first time. Jasmine could see May leaning over far too early—just the way Jasmine had during the jumping class—and then sitting up abruptly just before the jump.

May almost lost her seat after the first jump, but regained it just in time. She rode up to Corey and Outlaw. "What did I do wrong?" Jasmine heard her ask Corey.

Corey's answer surprised Jasmine. "I don't think you leaned forward far enough," Corey told May. "I think you should be flatter against Macaroni's neck."

Before she realized what she was doing, Jasmine joined the conversation. "That's not right, Corey," she said.

May and Corey looked at Jasmine in innocent surprise. "Why? What's wrong with my advice?" demanded Corey.

"You're supposed to stay in balance until just before the jump," explained Jasmine. "Then lean forward—not too far. You want to lean forward naturally, at the same moment when Macaroni gets ready for the jump."

"You know, I think you're right, Jazz,"

said May. She grinned impishly at Corey. "That's the last time I listen to you, Corey Takamura!"

Both Corey and Jasmine laughed. Corey was usually the first person May and Jasmine went to for help. It was really unlike her to be wrong.

May tried the jumps again. This time she leaned forward at the right moment, and Macaroni went over the jumps beautifully.

"Good job, May!" said Corey. "Now it's my turn again!" She cantered Outlaw toward the jump.

Jasmine watched May and Corey jump a few more times. There was no denying it—they were having a blast. May even did a little cowgirl whoop as she finished her third turn, which made Macaroni canter even more briskly.

Most importantly, Jasmine couldn't help noticing how much Outlaw loved jumping. His ears were perked straight up, and he sassily swished his tail back and forth. He was having the time of his life.

Jasmine started to feel hollow inside. She realized that if she never jumped again, Outlaw couldn't jump much, either.

He'd have to wait for Corey or May to take a turn on him.

He's my pony, thought Jasmine. I'm keeping him from something he loves to do.

After May and Corey had done a few more rounds, they rode over to the edge of the ring where Jasmine stood with Samurai. They both dismounted.

"Are you finished jumping?" asked Jasmine in amazement. The Pony Tails had only been practicing for a half hour.

May nodded. "Yup," she answered. "I, uh, just remembered something. I left the kitchen in a mess. I tried to make a super-huge triple-decker sandwich for lunch, and I forgot to clean up. Mom is probably ready to kill me by now."

Corey handed Outlaw's reins to Jasmine and took Samurai's reins back. "Don't you want to try jumping with Samurai again?" asked Jasmine.

Corey shook her head. "Nope," she said. "I promised to help Jack bathe a few dogs." Jack was Doc Tock's student assistant. "We're really swamped with patients," she added.

"See ya, Jazz, Corey," said May, walking off with Macaroni.

"See ya," echoed Corey, walking off with Samurai.

Jasmine was left alone in the schooling ring with Outlaw.

10 Jasmine Jumps Again

Jasmine took another look at the jumps in the ring. Once again, she remembered her fall last Wednesday. But then she started to really think about it. After all, she hadn't gotten hurt. She had just made a mistake.

She took a deep breath. Then another one.

"Mr. Grover?" she called.

Mr. Grover was still in the next ring with his student horse. Now, however, he appeared to be finished and was just leading the horse back to the stable. When he heard Jasmine, he quickly tied the horse to a post outside the stable and came over to her.

"What's up, Jasmine?" he asked gently.

Jasmine nervously smiled at him. "Well, I took a jumping class last Wednesday, and I had a little accident," she said.

"A lot of riders do fall," said Mr. Grover solemnly.

"I—I was thinking," stammered Jasmine. "I was thinking . . . of trying again. You see, I didn't get back on Outlaw right after my fall. Do you think you could help me?"

Mr. Grover nodded. "It's tough getting your confidence back. But I'm happy that you're willing to try again. That takes courage, Jasmine. I'd love to help."

Jasmine got back on Outlaw. Instead of directing her to go over the jumps already set up, Mr. Grover laid out some cavalletti on the ground.

Jasmine concentrated on riding over the cavalletti. She made sure that her heels were down, her grip on the reins was firm yet light, and her posture was upright.

"Terrific!" said Mr. Grover. "Are you ready for the real thing?"

He motioned toward the jumps.

Jasmine slowly turned Outlaw so that they faced the jumps.

Mr. Grover started talking. "Remember what I told you, Jasmine? It's like playing a duet together. You love Outlaw. He loves you. When you jump together, he's just waiting for you to tell him to do the right thing. Everything should be in harmony."

Jasmine nodded at Mr. Grover. Then she and Outlaw cantered toward the first jump. She made sure that her heels stayed down and her head stayed up.

As she approached the jump, Jasmine felt as if the fences were rushing at her in a blur. She could hear Outlaw's hooves pounding the ground. For a split second, Jasmine relived the fall. She could remember the awful, terrible moment when she lost her balance and fell to the ground.

Then she remembered what she was doing. She was riding Outlaw, her own pony. She knew how to ride Outlaw better than anyone else in the world. All Outlaw needed was the right guidance from her.

When they got to the jump, Jasmine leaned forward with the natural motion of

Outlaw's body. Although she had a firm grip on the reins, she gave Outlaw lots of room to extend his neck. She looked straight ahead.

Outlaw gathered himself and effortlessly cleared the first jump, then the second, and finally the third.

Jasmine couldn't stop a big grin from spreading all over her face. Mr. Grover chuckled. "You look like a totally different girl," he teased. "When you started toward the jump, you looked like you were going to the dentist! Now you look like you've just gotten a Christmas present!"

"I want to try again," said Jasmine eagerly.

"Be my guest," said Mr. Grover, smiling.

Jasmine and Outlaw took the jumps again, and then again. Mr. Grover, his eyes twinkling, walked over to the cavalleti and raised each one two inches. Now they were almost a foot off the ground.

"I think you're ready to handle these," he said. "You're doing great."

Jasmine reminded herself that she was still a long way from six-foot fences. Now she knew that it was important to learn everything she could about the low jumps before she attempted the big ones.

Best of all, she knew Outlaw was thrilled to be jumping with her. After each round, he couldn't wait to get back to the beginning of the course.

Jasmine and Outlaw took the higher jumps smoothly. Mr. Grover complimented Jasmine several times on her seat and balance. She wished Corey and May could see her jump.

Soon Jasmine's wish was granted. After a fourth successful round, she heard clapping and cheering from the side of the ring. May and Corey were back!

"Way to go, Jazz!" May called out.

"I have a new nickname for you," said Corey. "Jumping Jasmine!"

Jasmine turned a little pink, but she couldn't help being pleased. She rode over to May and Corey.

"I thought you had to clean up the kitchen," Jasmine said, looking at May.

"I was faster than lightning today!" grinned May.

Jasmine looked at Corey. "Corey, I thought you had to help Jack," she said.

Corey looked at her innocently. "Oh, he decided at the last minute that he didn't need my help," she answered.

"Anyway, what does it matter?" said May impatiently. "You did it, Jasmine! You jumped again!"

"I couldn't have done it without your dad's help," said Jasmine.

"No, I think you're wrong," said Mr. Grover's voice behind her. They turned and saw him standing there, smiling at them. "I think," he said to Jasmine, "you should thank your friends first."

Jasmine looked puzzled for a minute. Then the pieces of the puzzle started to fall into place. She remembered watching Corey jump with Outlaw and then realizing how much fun her pony was missing.

Then she remembered May's mysterious mistakes at jumping, and how Corey had given her the wrong advice. Both Corey and May were really good at jumping—had they messed up on purpose? Finally Jasmine recalled her friends' abrupt departures from the ring, and how Mr. Grover was suddenly free to help her.

"This was all a setup!" she said, looking accusingly at May and Corey.

"Yup," said May. She and Corey were looking pleased with themselves. Their plan had worked.

For a second Jasmine felt a flash of annoyance. She had been tricked into doing something she hadn't wanted to do. How pushy could her friends get?

Then she looked again at May and Corey. They were both beaming. Jasmine knew they were really happy that she was jumping again. They were happy for her. It didn't matter if it was a setup. It had worked!

Jasmine dismounted from Outlaw. Then she pulled May and Corey closer together and gave them both a big hug.

"You guys are the best," she said. "Thanks for your help."

"You would have done the same for us," answered Corey. "You really saved me when you helped me with that poster. My mom loves it."

"You've helped me so many times, I've lost track," said May.

The three Pony Tails led a tired Outlaw back to his stall. Jasmine, Corey, and May gave him an extra-special grooming to reward him for his hard work.

"A snack back at my house?" asked Jasmine, looking at May and Corey.

They didn't need any persuasion. The three girls jogged to Jasmine's house.

When they walked into the kitchen, Mr. James was doing the dishes. Mrs. James was just taking a sheet of oatmeal cookies from the oven, so Jasmine knew Sophie was probably taking a nap upstairs.

"Mom, Dad," said Jasmine excitedly, "I did it!"

Mr. and Mrs. James looked confused.

"Jasmine jumped again!" May told them.

"She was a real pro!" said Corey.

Mr. and Mrs. James smiled. Mr. James dried his hands and gave Jasmine a big hug. "That's great, Jazzie," he told her. "Your mom and I were worried that your fall shook you up—permanently."

Mrs. James also gave Jasmine a hug. "We don't want you to fall ever again, but we're proud that you learned about the dangers of jumping and then were able to put them behind you."

"You're going to be a great jumper," said Mr. James, pulling a curl of Jasmine's hair affectionately.

"I couldn't have done it without the help of my friends," Jasmine told him. "They helped me get over how scared I was to jump again."

"That's nothing," chimed in Corey. "Jasmine helps us all the time, too. We did a beautiful poster last week for my mom, and we couldn't have done it without Jazz's help!"

That reminded May of something. "Speaking of posters," she said, "where is that dinosaur chart you did for school, Jazz? We're dying to see it."

Mr. James put a hand to his forehead and groaned. "Okay, you guys are moving much too fast for me. Animal posters? Dinosaur charts? I thought we were talking about jumping!"

The Pony Tails giggled. As May and

86

Corey explained about the dinosaur chart, Jasmine ran upstairs and got it from her closet.

Mrs. James unrolled the chart and laid it out on the kitchen table. "Honey, this is incredible!" she exclaimed.

Mr. James bent down to take a closer look. "This is terrific, Jasmine. Why didn't you show it to us before?"

"You and Mom were so busy . . . ," started Jasmine. Then she stopped. She knew what her parents were about to say.

Mrs. James put an arm around Jasmine. "We are *never* too busy to look at your projects," she said to Jasmine. "Even though we may seem distracted at times, that doesn't mean we can't stop for a minute and admire our daughter's work."

"Everyone's got to stop and smell the roses once in a while," said Mr. James. Jasmine explained to May and Corey that this was her father's way of saying that he had gotten too wrapped up in his work lately.

Jasmine told her parents about the school art exhibition. Mr. and Mrs. James promised to come and to bring Sophie in her stroller. Then Mrs. James picked up the poster and carefully taped it to the kitchen wall.

"Now I can look at it every day and learn about dinosaurs until it's time for the school exhibition," she told Jasmine.

Jasmine looked at her poster again. She noticed the wrinkles on the edges of the chart, from when she'd stuffed the chart into her closet.

Somehow, though, she didn't mind the wrinkles. They reminded her that she sometimes made mistakes. They also reminded her that she could learn from her mistakes—especially with great friends like May and Corey.

Jasmine also knew that her parents were busy people, with two girls to care for and full-time careers. They could make mistakes, too—like forgetting to ask Jasmine about certain things. But they loved her, and she knew it.

"Are those cookies up for grabs?" Jasmine asked her mother, looking at the sheet of oatmeal cookies warm from the oven.

"Help yourselves," said Mrs. James, smiling. "I made them for you."

The Pony Tails started munching on oatmeal cookies. Mrs. James poured milk.

As for Jasmine, she could hardly wait to jump again. She said to May and Corey, "Let's try jumping again tomorrow."

May and Corey immediately agreed. The Pony Tails loved to find new activities. Now they could all jump—together.

Jasmine's
Jumping Tips

Max once told us that we can learn more from our mistakes than from the things we do right. As usual, he knew what he was talking about.

I learned some things about jumping from my friends, some things about jumping from Max, and some things about jumping from Mr. Grover. I even learned some things from my pony. Mostly, though, I learned by doing it myself—wrong—and then doing it right.

Maybe I can save *you* some trouble and bruises.

There are three basic parts to jumping: approach, takeoff, and landing. Each of them is as important as the other two and if I mess up in one of them, the whole jump will be a mess.

The approach sets the stage for everything else. I have to be completely balanced, not too far to one side or the other, not too far forward and not leaning back. That's a lot of *nots* to remember, but balance is really important for anything I do when I ride. Almost every exercise Max ever has us do relates to balance. It's a word I hear a lot. The more I hear it, the more I know it's important.

Next, I have to be sure my eyes are telling me where I'm going, because if I'm not sure where I'm going, Outlaw is definitely going to be confused! What that means is that I have to keep my eyes focused on the far side of the jump, not on the ground on this side of it—unless that's where I want to end up!

When it gets time for the takeoff, Outlaw has to do the work, but I have to tell him when and how to do it. I tell him the way I tell him almost everything—with my body. He can see the jump. I shift my seat back a little and lean forward at the same time. My weight is on the stirrups (balanced!) and my back is flat all the way from my hips to my neck. My head is head up (looking forward) and my legs are relaxed.

Then, just at the moment of the actual takeoff, I move my arms forward as Outlaw stretches his neck forward. That loosens the reins so Outlaw can lead with his head. That's called a release.

Then there's the finish. I'm as likely to end up in the dirt if I don't finish the jump properly, as I am if I don't start it right. Once Outlaw has his feet on the ground, I need to sit up straight again. That'll draw in the reins some and I can tighten them more if they need it. I also have to keep my eye on where I want to go (not where I've been) and never, ever lose my—you got it—balance.

Sounds easy, doesn't it? Well, like a lot of things that have to do with riding, there are approximately seventy-three things you have to do right all at once. Also, like other parts of riding, when you do all seventy-three the right way, it's wonderful!

There are a couple of other things I need to tell you about jumping. No matter how hard you study and how well you do all seventy-three things, you're going to make mistakes. If you don't, your pony will make mistakes. Mistakes on ponies usually end up with the rider on the ground. So, first, middle, last, and always: *Wear a helmet and have your chin strap fastened.* You can wear any kind of helmet you want as long as it has a label on the inside that says it's been approved by the ASTM/SEI. I just looked that up. What it stands for is American Society for Testing Materials and Safety Equipment Institute. What it means is that it will protect you.

Making mistakes is part of learning. Whenever anyone falls off a pony, people tell them to get back in the saddle. Everybody knows they're *supposed* to do that. What everybody doesn't think about when they tell you that is that it isn't easy. If you've just taken a tumble and if you hurt, it may be that the first thing you want to do is to run away and the last thing you want to do is to get back in the saddle. You might be angry with your pony. You are probably embarrassed. Maybe even ashamed. Forget that stuff. It's not important. What is important is getting back in the saddle. It helps remind you that it was fun and that you aren't really hurt. It also reminds your pony that you're the boss.

And I promise you that once you are back in the saddle, you'll remember what you did wrong. That's how I learn from my mistakes. You will, too.

Jasmine's Guide to Jumping

There are two kinds of jumping competition: hunter and jumper. What makes them different? In hunter jumping, the horse and rider are judged by how well they perform together. It doesn't matter how fast you go over the fences, but it does matter how you go over them. In other words, the judges are looking for even strides, manners, and jumping style. The course itself is usually very straightforward, but you have to jump the fences in a certain order. If you don't, you and your horse can be disqualified.

In jumping competitions you have to get over the fences quickly and cleanly—and stay on your horse, of course. Riders and horses jump high, wide fences—sometimes as much as five feet high and six feet wide. And they do it faster than in hunter competitions. To make it even harder, the fences are set up so that horses have to make tight turns to get from one fence to the next. Rider and horse really have to communicate well to get through one of these courses.

In show jumping, the fences are jumped in a certain order. If you don't jump fences in the right order, you are given penalty points, called *faults*. If your horse knocks down an obstacle, puts a hoof in the water at a water jump, or doesn't jump a fence at all, you get more faults. If that isn't enough to think about, a show jumper also has to complete the jump course in a set time or be assigned time faults. It's a lot to remember.

Both kinds of jumping competition are really exciting to watch, but I can't wait until the day when I can take part in a competition myself. I just know that Outlaw and I will make a great jumping team!

About the Author

Bonnie Bryant was born and raised in New York City, and she still lives there today. She spends her summers in a house on a lake in Massachusetts.

Ms. Bryant began writing about girls and horses when she started The Saddle Club series in 1987. So far there are more than fifty books in that series. Much as she likes telling the stories about Stevie, Carole, and Lisa, she decided that the younger riders at Pine Hollow, especially May Grover, have stories of their own that need telling. That's how Pony Tails was born.

Ms. Bryant rides horses when she has time away from her computer, but she doesn't have a horse of her own. She likes to ride different horses and enjoys a variety of riding experiences. She says she thinks most of her readers are much better riders than she is!

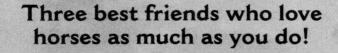